Reading Together at Home

THE STORY OF
CHICKEN
LICKEN

First U.S. paperback edition 1998

ISBN 0-7636-0535-2

4 6 8 10 9 7 5

Printed in Hong Kong

Candlewick Press
2067 Massachusetts Avenue
Cambridge, Massachusetts 02140

OH, TURKEY LURKEY, DON'T GO!
I was going and I met Goose Loose,
and Goose Loose met Drake Lake,
and Drake Lake met Duck Luck,
and Duck Luck met Cock Lock,
and Cock Lock met Henny Penny,
and Henny Penny met
Chicken Licken and the sky
had fallen on her poor little head.
Now we are going to tell the king.

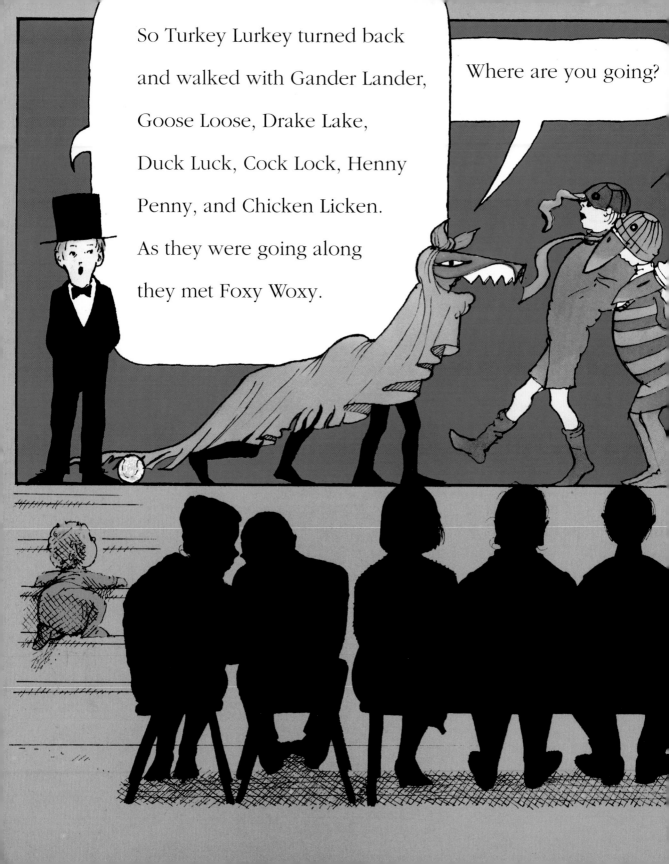

Foxy Woxy took them

into the fox's hole.

He and his young ones

soon ate up poor Chicken Licken,

Henny Penny, Cock Lock, Duck Luck,

Drake Lake, Goose Loose,

Gander Lander, and Turkey Lurkey.

So they never saw the king

and they never told him

that the sky had fallen.

Read it again

School play

You can use the front page picture of the stage, the curtains, and the audience to talk about the fact that this is the story of a school play. You may like to use different voices for the characters as you read and point to whoever is speaking.

Baby stories

Children can tell the story of the baby, which is told in the pictures, not in words. Look at each picture in order and describe what happens. You could tell stories about your child as a baby, using photographs, and make a photo album about the first adventures you both remember.

Play a part

Once you've read this story aloud several times, you could invite your child to read a part. A good way to start is with the speech bubble in the middle of each page: "I am going to the woods for some food." Encourage your child to put on different voices to suit each character.

I'm Foxy Woxy and I've got a deep voice.

Different journeys

This is a story where one character sets off on a journey and meets others along the way. Children can make up their own story using the same pattern about a journey to the park, the store, or school, where they meet friends, animals, or story characters. You could write it down together in a book with pictures of all the different characters.

One day Katey Latey went to the park and a chestnut fell on her poor little head. Oh no! The moon has fallen. I will go and tell the king. So Katey Latey turned back and met Jack Sack.

Make a puppet

Together, try making simple sock puppets, paper masks, or hats for each character. Children can use these to act out the story with friends, with brothers or sisters, with you, or on their own.

They can also use them to make up their own stories about the characters.

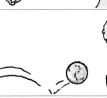

Reading and Writing

If you and your child have enjoyed reading this book together, you may also enjoy writing about it together. Shared writing, like shared reading, is a wonderful way to help develop children's early literacy skills. Encourage children to write or draw their own version of the story, their feelings toward the story, or an experience from their life that relates to the story in some way. You may wish to paste their work on these two pages as a keepsake and a record of their literacy development. Children not yet ready to write may enjoy dictating a story for you to write down for them. For more information and ideas about writing and reading with your child, please see the *Reading Together at Home Parents' Handbook.*

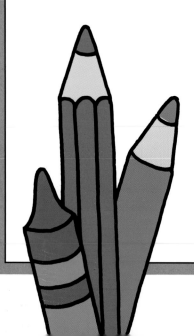

Reading Together at Home
Green Level: Taking Off

How this book helps support your child's reading development:

This is a traditional nursery story that some children will know. *The Story of Chicken Licken* introduces a new form of storytelling— it is told as a play, using speech bubbles. The simple, strongly patterned text helps children build up their confidence and stamina as readers, enabling them to read it independently fairly quickly. The illustrations tell stories additional to the one told through words—children can follow the events shown in the silhouettes and recount the baby's story. They can also enjoy guessing the audience's conversations. Silhouettes are a different type of illustration that children might not have seen before. This version of *Chicken Licken* encourages children to act out the story, helping them understand and remember it more readily.

See the *Reading Together at Home Parents' Handbook* for more information on specific reading skills your child is developing as he or she reads books in the Taking Off level of the *Reading Together at Home* series.